OWEN
TO THE RESCUE

JURASSIC WORLD™

MVFOL

ADAPTED BY MEREDITH RUSU

FROM THE SCREENPLAY BY JEREMY ADAMS. STORY BY DAVID SHAYNE.

SCHOLASTIC INC.

ISBN 978-1-338-53920-2

10 9 8 7 6 5 4 3 2 1   19 20 21 22 23
Printed in the U.S.A.   40

First printing 2019

Book design by Jess Meltzer

Welcome to Jurassic World, a theme park
with the most powerful dinosaurs ever!
Jurassic World sits on a big island.

Simon Masrani is the excitable owner of Jurassic World.

"We're going to open a new exhibit tonight!" he tells everyone. "A *secret* exhibit with three new dinosaurs!"

Masrani puts the smart Claire Dearing in charge of getting the three new dinosaurs to the island on time.

She has a cool animal trainer helping her. His name is Owen Grady.

Owen brings the three dinosaurs for
the secret exhibit to Jurassic World on a
helicopter. He also brings four Raptor eggs.

"Keep an eye on those eggs, Red," Owen
tells his pet dog. "They're precious cargo."

When Owen arrives on the island, the Raptor eggs hatch. One of the Raptors lets Owen pet her!

"Would you look at that!" Owen smiles. "They decided to come out and join the fun!"

Vic Hoskins is the head of security at Jurassic World. "You have a way with those dinosaurs," Vic tells Owen. "Ever thought about working here?"

"Nah," says Owen. "I'm just here to deliver the dinosaurs. Then I'm off!"

That's when Claire tells Owen his job isn't finished.

"You were supposed to deliver the dinosaurs to the *other* side of the island," she says. "So, if you want to get paid, you'll have to get a move on."

Owen starts to follow Claire. But suddenly, he spots a little boy playing in one of the park's Gyrospheres—clear, rolling balls that let visitors see the dinosaurs up close.

"Uh, I don't think you should do that!" Owen shouts.

But the kid doesn't listen. He speeds off!

No one sees the boy race away other than Owen.

That means Owen is the only one who can save the kid before he becomes a dinosaur's lunch! Yikes!

"Come on, Red!" Owen calls to his dog. "If I can get close, I can pull in front and slow the Gyrosphere down!"

Owen and Red stop the Gyrosphere just before it rolls off a cliff. The little boy is safe! But Owen is in trouble. A T. rex has already spotted him!

"Sorry, Miss T. rex, but I don't feel much like getting eaten right now," Owen says nervously.

Just when the T. rex is about to chomp, one of the baby Raptors sees that Owen is in danger. She pulls Owen up to safety using a vine.

"You just saved my life!" Owen says in amazement. "Thank you!"

Little does Owen know, his troubles aren't over yet.

A worker named Danny Nedermeyer is up to no good. Danny really dislikes Simon Masrani and Jurassic World. And he plans to wreck the park—he wants it shut down for good!

When no one is looking, Danny uses a computer to open the roof to the building where all the flying dinosaurs live. A Pteranodon escapes and swoops out into the park!

Vic is giving Owen a ride back to base in a helicopter when an alarm siren blares. "Emergency!" a worker warns over the radio. "A Pteranodon has gotten loose!"

But it's too late. The Pteranodon smashes into the helicopter and stalls the engine.

"We need to kick-start the blades or we're going to crash!" Owen cries.

Thinking fast, he leaps from the helicopter, grabs on to the Pteranodon's legs, and kicks the blades of the helicopter so they spin again.

Owen's plan works! The helicopter starts back up!

Vic is impressed. "You *really* have a way with those dinosaurs, kid!"

Safe and sound back at base, Owen meets up with Claire.

"So, you finally decided to show back up and finish your job?" she asks.

"Are you kidding?" Owen exclaims. "Do you know what I just went through?!"

"I'm on a major time crunch," Claire insists. "If I don't get these three dinosaurs to their exhibit in time for the opening tonight, Simon will be furious!"

"Okay, here's the deal," Owen tells her. "I'll get you to the exhibit on time. But after that, I get paid."

Claire nods. "Deal."

Owen studies the map. "I think I see a shortcut that could save us some time," he says.

He steers them off the main road . . . and accidently crashes into a T. rex pen!

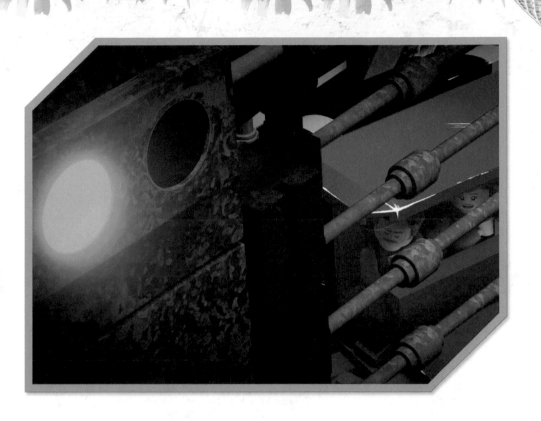

"That was close!" Claire exclaims. "But it's okay. As long as the light on the pen stays green, we're safe. The T. rex can't escape."

Unfortunately, Danny is still up to his mischief. With a few taps on the keyboard, he unlocks the T. rex pen and releases the dinosaur!

"AHHHHHHH!" scream Owen and Claire.

The T. rex flips their truck over! The three dinosaurs for the exhibit escape, but Claire and Owen are trapped. They're in REAL trouble now!

"We have to get out of here!" Claire cries.
"I have an idea!" Owen tells her. He uses
the broken pieces of the truck to build a
getaway car. "Hold on tight!" he yells.

"There's only one way to deal with a grumpy dino," says Owen. "And that's a time-out!"

Owen aims a net cannon on the back of the getaway car at the T. rex and fires!

Bull's-eye! Owen's shot is a direct hit. The T. rex gets tangled in the net.

"Where do you want her?" Owen cheerfully asks Claire.

Claire shakes her head. "That was unbelievable. Are you *sure* you don't want to work here? You really have a way with dinos!"

Up in the control room, Danny is spotted by Masrani.

"What are you doing?" Masrani demands.

"Uh, nothing," Danny fibs. "Just . . . fixing your copier."

Masrani stares for a long moment. "Oh, good!" he says. "It's been broken for weeks!"

While Masrani is distracted, Danny slips away. He'll continue his mischief another day.

Later that night, Owen and Claire watch with the crowd as Masrani unveils the park's secret exhibit.

"I give you the Dino Carousel!" Masrani announces.

"THAT'S the secret exhibit?" Owen asks in disbelief. "I almost became a T. rex's dinner twice for a Dino Carousel?!"

Claire shrugs. "Masrani did say it was a surprise . . . Well, weren't you surprised?"

"Yeah," Owen says. "A little TOO surprised!"

The next day, Owen has a surprise of his own for Claire and Vic.

"I've decided to work here at Jurassic World after all," he tells them. "Training these rascals has kind of grown on me. And after yesterday's adventure, how much crazier could anything get?"